AF594178

## A Note to Parents

Feel free to share *The First Christmas* with children not only during the Christmas season, but also throughout the year; this book can be a special book at any time. As you prepare to give gifts, remember that the wise men brought gifts for Jesus. Instead of concentrating on what gifts children will receive, ask them what they plan to give to others and help them anticipate how happy the gift will make the other person. And if you have the opportunity, arrange to visit a small baby. Read stories about Jesus as a man and talk about how he was the baby that we remember at Christmas.

— *Delia Halverson*

Delia Halverson is the consultant for *Family Time Bible Stories*. An interdenominational lecturer on Christian education, she has written seven books, including *How Do Our Children Grow?*

*Scripture sources:* ***Luke* 1: 26-34 2:1-20 *Matthew* 2:1-12**

Family Time
Bible
Stories

# The First Christmas

*Retold by* Patricia Daniels

*Illustrated by* Sue Ellen Brown

Time Life for Children®
Alexandria, Virginia

Long, long ago, there was a little town called Nazareth. Nazareth lay in low, rolling hills a day's journey from the sea. In this quiet town lived a quiet young woman named Mary and a man named Joseph.

One day, as Mary sat sewing, the room filled with a clear, yet colorful light, like the inside of a diamond. In this light stood the angel Gabriel.

Mary was frightened, but Gabriel smiled kindly.

"Don't be afraid, Mary," he said. "God has chosen you to have a special child. You will name him Jesus, and he will be called the son of God."

"I will do as God says," said Mary.

And with a whoosh! of his great wings the angel disappeared.

Months passed as Mary waited for her special baby to be born. One day, Mary and Joseph had to go to the town of Bethlehem, many miles away. Together they packed clothes and food onto the back of Joseph's donkey, Susannah. On a windy morning they set out.

The journey took three long, dusty days. Mary rode on the donkey's back. Joseph walked beside them. Susannah kept her head down and thought about a warm stable at the end of the journey. As the third day darkened into night, they saw the lights of Bethlehem ahead.

"Joseph," said Mary, "I think the baby's coming."

Joseph could see that many people were visiting Bethlehem. He went to the first inn that he saw.

"Innkeeper," he said to the man who opened the door, "please find us a room for the night. We are tired and expecting a baby."

But the innkeeper just shook his head. "There is no room at this inn," he said. "Nor at any other inn in Bethlehem."

The innkeeper was right. Joseph and Mary went from inn to inn, but there was no room for them. Then Susannah snorted and nudged Joseph with her nose. The donkey led them to a stable at the edge of town.

The stable door was open. The cows and sheep inside looked at them with friendly brown eyes. Joseph helped Mary lie down on a bed of straw.

And it was there in a stable, on a starry night, that Mary gave birth to a beautiful boy. She and Joseph loved him.

They wrapped the baby in bands of cloth so he would feel warm and safe. Then they laid him in the animals' manger to sleep.

Outside, in the grassy hills around Bethlehem, shepherds huddled in their coats and watched their sheep.

Suddenly, an angel appeared in the sky. Light shone on the surprised faces of the shepherds.

"I bring you good news!" said the angel in a singing voice. "Today the promised child has been born. You will find him lying in a manger, wrapped in bands of cloth."

And the angel was joined in the starry sky by other glorious angels singing praises to God.

When the angels had gone, the shepherds hurried down from the hills to the tiny stable. There they saw the child resting in the straw.

"Father!" said the first shepherd boy. "The baby smiled at me!" The boy smiled back, his heart filled with happiness. Then he took his father's hand and left to spread the joyful news through the town.

As the days passed, people in Bethlehem and beyond began to hear about the holy child. Mary, Joseph, and the baby moved into a small house and received many visitors.

One night they had the most amazing guests of all: three wise men on camelback, bringing presents of gold and perfumes for the growing child.

"How did you find us?" Mary asked the wise men.

"We were told to follow the great star," they answered, pointing to the sky.

Mary and Joseph looked up. It was true—a splendid star lit up the sky above their house.

"What is the baby's name?" the wise men asked.

"Jesus," said Mary and Joseph proudly.

Jesus Christ grew up to be a great teacher who would tell people about faith and love. To this day, 2,000 years later, people around the world celebrate his birthday on Christmas.

**TIME-LIFE FOR CHILDREN®**

**Staff for FAMILY TIME BIBLE STORIES**

| | |
|---|---|
| Managing Editor: | Patricia Daniels |
| *Art Director:* | Susan K. White |
| *Publishing Associate:* | Marike van der Veen |
| *Editorial Assistant:* | Mary M. Saxton |
| *Copy Editor:* | Colette Stockum |
| *Production Manager:* | Marlene Zack |
| *Quality Assurance Manager:* | Miriam Newton |



First printing. Printed in U.S.A. Published simultaneously in Canada.

Time Life Inc. is a wholly owned subsidiary of THE TIME INC. BOOK COMPANY.

TIME-LIFE is a trademark of Time Warner Inc. U.S.A.
School and library distribution by Time-Life Education,
P.O. Box 85026, Richmond, VA 23285-5026.
For subscription information, call 1-800-621-7026.

*Library of Congress Cataloging-in-Publication Data*

Daniels, Patricia, 1955- The first Christmas / retold by Patricia Daniels; illustrated by Sue Ellen Brown. p. cm.—(Family time Bible stories) Summary: Retells the story of the birth of Jesus, from the journey to Bethlehem to the arrival of the three kings. ISBN 0-7835-4625-4 1. Jesus Christ—Nativity—Juvenile literature. 2. Bible stories, English—N.T. Gospels. [1. Jesus Christ—Nativity. 2. Bible stories—N.T. 3. Christmas.] I. Brown, Sue Ellen. II. Title. III. Series.
BT315.2.D36 1995 95-36899
232.92'1— dc20 CIP
AC